This book belongs to

Copyright © 2014

make believe ideas ltd

The Wilderness, Berkhamsted, Hertfordshire, HP4 2AZ, UK.

www.makebelieveideas.com

Written by Tim Bugbird.
Illustrated by Lara Ede.
Designed by Ellie Fahy.

Molly the Muffin Fairy

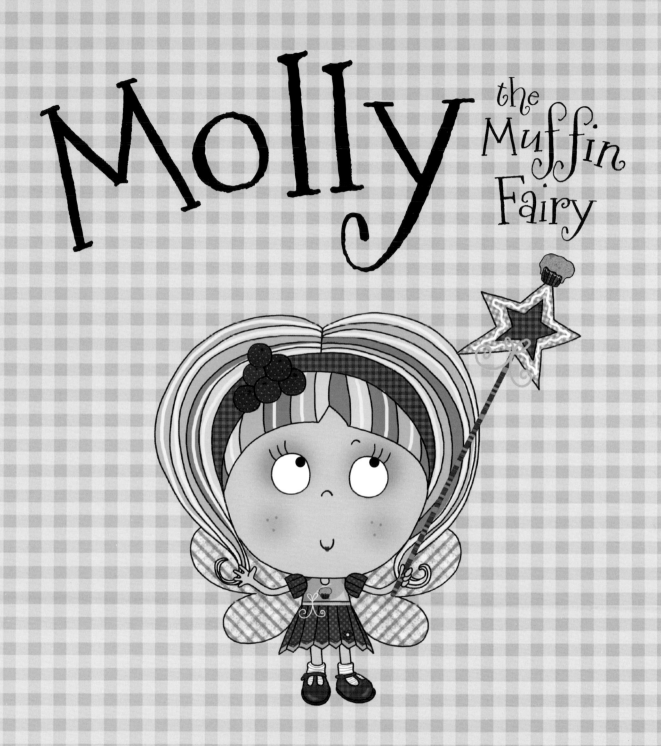

Tim Bugbird · Lara Ede

make
believe
ideas

Molly the Muffin Fairy was famous in Fairyland for making perfect muffins — some small and some quite grand.

Each one was baked 'til **spongy**,
golden, soft and sweet.
Her wand put in big **blueberries**
to make the **treats** complete!

The blueberries came in boxes, delivered by Mel and Kerri — her two best friends, who drove a truck shaped like a giant berry!

But then one day when **baking**,
Molly's temper began to **fray**;

her **muffins** had no softness —
she was having a **bad** bake day!

Her baking got **no better** and soon **Molly's** fairy home was full of **rubbery muffins** with tops as hard as **stone!**

Molly was not happy. The baking was making her MAD!
She fussed and fumed and finally flipped!
What she did was really bad . . . .

She grabbed a tray of **muffins** and **threw** them to the floor,

then took a **muffin** in her hand and **hurled** it out the door!

The muffin hit her trampoline and bounced up in the air.

The strangest scene there's **ever** been

followed on from there . . .

and pinged
and ponged,

It bounced
and bumped

startling a **squirrel**,
who scampered and woke
a **porcupine** down below!

flying
to and fro,

Up with a **start**, the porcupine **ran**
to find a **safe place** to hide.

But he **poked** the edge of Molly's pool –
his **spikes** making **holes** in the side!

Water gushed out from the holes,
flooding the road all around.

Then Mel and Kerri's truck arrived,
but **how** would they cross the **wet** ground?

Molly cried, "It's all a mess!"
Mel said, "Do stop whining!
Those muffins of yours could help us —
every cloud has a silver lining!"

"Maybe they could make a **path**. Have a go and see."
So Molly laid the **muffins** down . . . .

and the truck
crossed **easily!**

Then, before the **fairies'** eyes, the **muffins** began to expand.

Soaking up water, the bakes became the biggest in Fairyland!

"The muffins feel soft!" cried Molly. "But don't eat them; they're not clean!

Though squashed together, I think they'll make . . ."

Molly learnt that when things look bad, you can always find a way to see things from the **sunny side** and turn around your day!